NICK JR
Blue's Clues

My Visit with Periwinkle

D1507397

by Alison Inches
illustrated by David B. Levy

Ready-to-Read

Simon Spotlight/Nick Jr.

New York   London   Toronto   Sydney   Singapore

Based on the TV series *Blue's Clues*® created by Traci Paige Johnson, Todd Kessler, and Angela C. Santomero as seen on Nick Jr.® On *Blue's Clues,* Joe is played by Donovan Patton. Photos by Joan Marcus.

SIMON SPOTLIGHT
An imprint of Simon & Schuster Children's Publishing Division
1230 Avenue of the Americas, New York, New York 10020
Copyright © 2003 Viacom International Inc. All rights reserved.
NICKELODEON, NICK JR., *Blue's Clues*, and all related titles, logos, and characters are trademarks of Viacom International Inc.
All rights reserved, including the right of reproduction in whole or in part in any form.
READY-TO-READ, SIMON SPOTLIGHT, and colophon are registered trademarks of Simon & Schuster.
Manufactured in the United States of America
First Edition
2 4 6 8 10 9 7 5 3

Library of Congress Cataloging-in-Publication Data
Inches, Alison.
My visit with Periwinkle / by Alison Inches.—1st ed.
p. cm.—(Ready-to-read ; #7)
Summary: Blue and Periwinkle the cat get together for lunch and some fun in the park.
ISBN 0-689-85230-4
[1. Friendship—Fiction. 2. Dogs—Fiction. 3. Cats—Fiction]
I. Levy, David B. - ill. II. Title. III. Series.
PZ7.I355My 2003
[E]—dc21
2002006114

Hi! It is me, .
BLUE
Today PERIWINKLE is
coming to my HOUSE
for a visit.

When gets
here, we will have
 , , and  .

Then we are going to play in the .

PARK

I made a  of
things to do before

 comes over.

PERIWINKLE

1. Clean the .
HOUSE

2. Make .
SANDWICHES

3. Put out and .
MILK   COOKIES

First we have to clean
the  HOUSE .

I need to put away my  . I have RED blocks and BLUE blocks.

BLOCKS

RED

BLUE

While Joe makes the 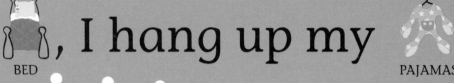 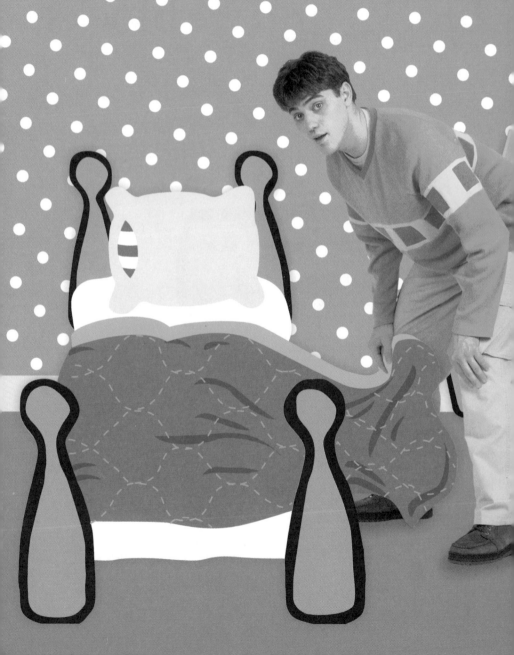, I hang up my

BED

PAJAMAS

They have ⭐ on them!

STARS

The  is clean.

HOUSE

Now it is time to
make the  .
SANDWICHES

TO DO LIST
1. 🏠 ✓
2. 🥪 —
3. 🍪🥛—

and help me

MR. SALT   MRS. PEPPER

 likes 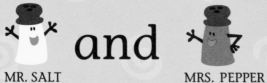 .

PERIWINKLE   PEANUT BUTTER   SANDWICHES

I like  .

CHEESE SANDWICHES

Almost done!
What is the last
thing on my ?

LIST

Put out MILK and COOKIES !

The have
COOKIES · HEARTS

on them.

They make us smile.

PERIWINKLE is at the **DOOR** !

He brought  KITES for us to fly at the park.

We can fly our 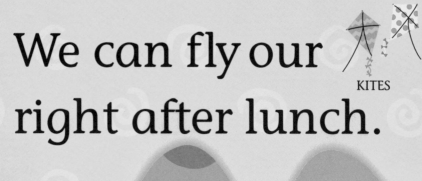 KITES right after lunch.

The  make
COOKIES
smile too!

PERIWINKLE

Look at our  **KITES** flying in the sky! I love when **PERIWINKLE** visits.